SOCCER
SUSPICIONS

BY JAKE MADDOX

text by
Bryan Patrick Avery

STONE
a capstone imprint

Published by Stone Arch Books, an imprint of Capstone
1710 Roe Crest Drive, North Mankato, Minnesota 56003
capstonepub.com

Library of Congress Cataloging-in-Publication Data
Names: Maddox, Jake, author. | Avery, Bryan Patrick, author.
Title: Soccer suspicions / Jake Maddox ; text by Bryan Patrick Avery.
Description: North Mankato, Minnesota : Stone Arch Books, an imprint of Capstone, 2022.
| Series: Jake Maddox JV mysteries | Audience: Ages 8–11. | Audience: Grades 4–6. |
Summary: Seventh grader Gabriella Carter, goalie for Stratford Park Middle School, was
given the treasured medal of professional soccer star Shaune Covington to hold for a week,
but now it has disappeared from her backpack. Clearly somebody took it, and it is up to
Gabriella and her friends to gather clues, check alibis, and figure out who took the precious
medal—and why.
Identifiers: LCCN 2021033228 (print) | LCCN 2021033229 (ebook) | ISBN 9781663975171
(hardcover) | ISBN 9781666330021 (paperback) | ISBN 9781666330038 (pdf)
Subjects: LCSH: Soccer stories. | Medals—Juvenile fiction. | Theft—Juvenile fiction. |
Detective and mystery stories. | CYAC: Mystery and detective stories. | Soccer—Fiction. |
Medals—Fiction. | Stealing—Fiction. | LCGFT: Detective and mystery fiction.
Classification: LCC PZ7.M25643 Son 2022 (print) | LCC PZ7.M25643 (ebook) | DDC 813.6
[Fic]—dc23
LC record available at https://lccn.loc.gov/2021033228
LC ebook record available at https://lccn.loc.gov/2021033229

Designer: Heidi Thompson

Image Credits: Newscom: Blend Images/Kris Timken, cover

Printed and bound in the USA.   4608

TABLE OF CONTENTS

CHAPTER I

DRILLS

Near the end of her final warm-up lap, Gabriella Carter started to sprint. She was determined to finish first. No one expected the goalie to be the fastest player on the soccer team, but Gabriella felt she needed to work hard to prove herself to her teammates.

The Stratford Park Middle School Pelicans soccer team was one of the best in the region. They had won the league championship the year before, and many of the current starters had seen plenty of playing time during that championship season. This year, the entire starting lineup was made up of eighth graders who had helped the Pelicans win the title.

All except for Gabriella. Gabriella was in seventh grade and in her first year on the team. She had beaten out Neveah Williams, an eighth grader, for the starting goalie position. There were a few grumbles from her teammates at first. But once they saw how hard she worked, Gabriella won them over. Neveah had become her biggest supporter.

After twelve games, the Pelicans were undefeated and just one win away from another championship. Gabriella hadn't given up a goal all season.

Coach Wilson blew her whistle.

"Nice hustle, girls," she called. "Let's split up for drills."

Neveah grabbed a ball, and Gabriella followed her to the goal.

"Okay," Gabriella said. "Diving or sliding?"

"Diving," Neveah said with a laugh. "Let's get it out of the way."

Gabriella grinned.

"You first," Gabriella said.

Neveah tossed her the ball and stood in front of the goal.

"Ready?" Gabriella asked.

Neveah crouched and bounced on the balls of her feet.

"Ready," she said.

Gabriella tossed the ball to Neveah, just out of her reach. Neveah dove for the ball, caught it, and cradled it. She jumped up and tossed the ball back to Gabriella.

Gabriella caught the ball and quickly tossed it again. Neveah dove again and snatched the ball out of the air.

They went faster and faster until Neveah finally dove for a ball and missed. The ball flew past her and into the goal.

"*OOFF!*" Neveah landed hard.

"Your turn," she groaned from her spot on the ground.

Gabriella helped her up.

"That was fourteen in a row," Gabriella said. "Nice job!"

"Thanks," Neveah said. "What's your record? Thirty?"

Gabriella laughed. "I wish."

The girls switched sides and repeated the drill. Neveah tossed the ball, and Gabriella dove to catch it.

Neveah tossed the ball faster each time. Eventually, Gabriella dove for a ball and it glanced off her fingers and into the goal.

"That was twenty-four!" Neveah said. "That's got to be a record."

"Maybe a Pelicans record," Gabriella said as she stood up. "I bet a pro like Shaune Covington could get all the way to fifty."

"Do you think she does this same drill?" Neveah asked.

Gabriella nodded.

"My dad took me to a Capitol City FC game last year," she said. "We went early so we could watch warm-ups. She did all the same drills we do."

"Probably better though," Neveah said.

"Better and faster," Gabriella said. "She made everything look so easy."

"I was so excited when they won the U.S. Cup," Neveah said. "And all because of her."

"Six clean sheets in a row," Gabriella said. "She didn't give up a goal for the whole tournament."

Coach Wilson blew her whistle, and the girls lined up for their next drill.

Neveah stood in goal, and Gabriella tried to roll the ball past her. Neveah slid in front of the ball, grabbed it, and jumped back up.

"Can I tell you a secret?" Gabriella asked.

Gabriella rolled the ball again. Neveah slid and stopped it. She jumped back up and walked toward Gabriella.

"Of course," Neveah said.

"I have Shaune's medal from the U.S. Cup," Gabriella said. "It's in my backpack."

"WHAT!" Neveah yelled.

Coach Wilson turn to look at them. "Those drills aren't going to run themselves," she shouted.

Neveah got back in goal, and Gabriella rolled another ball to her.

"I don't get to keep it," Gabriella explained. "I just have it for the week as part of Capitol City FC's youth outreach program. My dad signed me up online, and I got picked. I get to keep the medal for a week."

"That's so cool," Neveah said. "Why is it secret?"

"I haven't told anybody yet," Gabriella said. "Plus, there's something else. Shaune is coming to our game on Friday."

Neveah's eyes widened.

"That's the real surprise," Gabriella said. "She said she'd stay after the game and take pictures with the team."

Coach Wilson blew her whistle.

"Goalies!" she shouted. "Do I need to come over there?"

"No!" Gabriella and Neveah shouted.

The girls went back to their drills.

"Ready to switch?" Neveah asked.

Gabriella didn't answer. She just stared across the field. A girl dressed in gray from head to toe walked across the field toward them.

"Who is that?" Neveah asked.

"Serena Satterfield," Gabriella said.

Serena held up a backpack and grinned.

"Did we switch backpacks again?" Gabriella asked.

Serena nodded.

"Just toss it over by the bench, please," Gabriella said. "Yours is over there."

"There's a problem," Serena said.

"What's wrong?" Gabriella asked.

"You remember the medal in your backpack?" Serena asked.

"Yes," Gabriella said. "It belongs to Shaune Covington. Wait, how do you know about the medal?"

Serena blushed.

"I opened your backpack," she explained. "That's how I figured out it wasn't mine. I saw the little bag inside. I was curious, so I opened it. Sorry."

"I guess that's okay," Gabriella said.

Serena frowned.

"So, the thing is," she said. "The medal's not there anymore."

CHAPTER 2

PROBLEMS

"What do you mean it's not there?" Gabriella asked, reaching for her bag.

Serena handed her the backpack. Gabriella dumped the backpack out on the ground and rummaged through the pile.

"No, no, no," she said. "What happened to it?"

"I don't know," Serena said. "I realized I had the wrong bag when I was at the robotics lab after school. We must have switched them after the assembly this afternoon."

"Wait," Neveah interrupted, "are you telling me that you two both have one of these hard-to-miss backpacks?"

She held up the empty backpack. The body of the backpack was purple with green and gold stripes. The straps were bright red.

"My dad thought it would be hard to lose track of," Gabriella said.

"My mom thought the same thing," Serena said. "It was supposed to be unique."

"Instead," Gabriella added, "we've spent the year accidentally switching backpacks."

"Is there something I need to know about?" Coach Wilson asked.

The girls had been so engrossed in their conversation they hadn't noticed her walk up behind them. Gabriella quickly stuffed everything into her backpack.

"Can I be excused for a few minutes?" she asked. "It's an emergency."

Coach Wilson frowned as she looked at each one of the girls. Then she nodded.

"Make it quick," she said. "I want to have a scrimmage today, and I can't do that with only one goalie."

"I'll hurry," Gabriella said. "I just need to run to the robotics lab with Serena."

Coach Wilson's eyebrows shot up in surprise, but she didn't respond. Gabriella and Serena hurried away before she could ask any questions.

The robotics lab was mostly deserted when Gabriella and Serena got there. Gabriella followed Serena into the observation area, a small room outside the main workshop.

"Where is everybody?" Gabriella asked.

"We had a short day today," Serena explained. "The team finished work on the new robot yesterday, so today was mostly a cleanup day."

"I see," Gabriella said. "Where was my backpack?"

Serena pointed to a group of shelves along the wall.

"It was on the middle shelf, down by the end," Serena said. "There's a label on the shelf with my name on it."

Gabriella found Serena's name and looked at the shelf. It was bare.

"There's nothing here," Gabriella said. "I don't even see anywhere it could have fallen out."

"I know," Serena said. "I don't think the medal fell out of your backpack. I think someone stole it."

Gabriella opened her mouth to say something, but words failed her.

"I know it sounds crazy," Serena said. "But it's the only explanation."

Gabriella looked around the room.

"Okay," she said. "Tell me what you remember."

"After the assembly, I grabbed my backpack," Serena said. "It was really your backpack, but I didn't realize that until later. I came straight here. I needed to get pictures of the team and wanted to get the camera set up."

She walked across the room to a small locker.

"We keep supplies locked up in here. Paint, old circuit boards, and, of course, the camera equipment. I got out the camera and set it up in the workshop. That's the room in there."

Serena pointed to a large room next to the observation area. The two rooms were separated by a glass wall.

"When did you figure out that you had my backpack?" Gabriella asked.

"Right after I set up the camera," Serena said. "I went to grab a snack out of my backpack. As soon as I opened the pack, I saw the blue velvet bag on top. I was surprised, so . . ."

"So you opened the bag," Gabriella said.

Serena sighed. "As soon as I saw the medal, I knew that backpack had to be yours," she said. "So I put it back in the bag and put the bag in the backpack."

Serena stopped talking when a girl called out from the workshop.

"Serena," the girl called. "Did you get pictures of all the finished circuitry?"

"Yes, Mia," Serena said. "I did."

Serena blew out a long breath.

"That's Mia," she said. "She's the robotics team captain. She can be a bit intense."

Gabriella looked up at the clock on the wall and realized she'd been away from practice for too long.

"I have to go!" she told Serena. "Is there anything else you can tell me?"

Serena shook her head.

"Sorry," she said. "I was busy taking pictures. I didn't even realize the medal was gone until I got ready to bring the backpack to you."

"Serena!" Mia called.

Serena sighed.

"I'd better go," she said. "If I think of anything else, I'll let you know."

CHAPTER 3

SCRIMMAGE

Gabriella made it back to the soccer field just as the team was getting ready to scrimmage.

"I'm glad you made it back," Coach Wilson said. "I was worried I would have to play goalie."

"Sorry, Coach," Gabriella said. "I didn't mean to be gone that long."

"Well, you're here now," Coach Wilson said. "Hustle up and get in position."

Gabriella sprinted across the field to her goal and

performed her pregame ritual. She touched the left post, then the right. Then she jumped up and tapped the crossbar. She did the same thing before the start of every game.

Coach Wilson blew her whistle, and Gabriella's side kicked off. Nima kicked a long pass down the left side of the field. Gemma caught it with her chest and dribbled toward the goal. Alexa, playing defense, raced forward and made a sliding tackle, kicking the ball away.

The two sides went back and forth, but no one got a good scoring chance. Nima dribbled the ball across midfield and passed to Gemma to start another attack. As Gabriella watched the back-and-forth action, her mind started to wander.

Who took the medal? she wondered. *How will I tell Shaune I lost it?*

"Incoming!" A shout interrupted Gabriella's thoughts.

Gabriella looked up and saw Layla racing toward

her on a breakaway. She had somehow gotten past the defenders. Gabriella knew she should have gone out to meet the ball and cut off the angle, but it was too late. She'd have to stay on her line and defend from there.

Layla faked left, and Gabriella started to lean that way. When she did, Layla straightened up and kicked the ball to the right. As Gabriella dove in the wrong direction, she could only watch as the ball sailed into the goal behind her.

Layla threw her arms into the air and screamed. "Gooooaaaaalllll!"

Coach Wilson blew her whistle.

"Quit daydreaming out there, Gabriella!" she shouted.

"Sorry," Gabriella called back.

Gabriella's side kicked off again. Gemma and Nima passed the ball back and forth several times but couldn't break through the defense. Nima passed the ball all the way back to Gabriella.

Gabriella received the pass and looked downfield for a place to make a long pass. She was so distracted, she didn't notice Layla racing toward her.

"Look out!" Gemma called.

It was too late. Gabriella tried to kick the ball away from Layla but missed. Layla tackled the ball away, and Gabriella could only watch as the ball rolled into her goal.

Coach Wilson blew her whistle and shook her head.

"Let's go again," she said.

Gabriella tried her best to focus on the scrimmage, but losing the medal occupied her thoughts. She let in two more goals that normally would have been easy saves for her. After the last goal, Coach Wilson's whistle shrieked.

"Bring it in," she ordered.

The team gathered around Coach Wilson.

"Okay, team," she said. "We have a big game coming up on Friday. We play the Moton Marauders. If we win, we clinch the league title."

The girls cheered.

"Don't celebrate too early," Coach Wilson warned. "We'll need to play well to win. That means we need intensity, drive, and," she looked at Gabriella, "focus."

Gabriella felt her face get hot. She knew Coach Wilson was right. She couldn't let easy goals get past her if the Pelicans were going to win.

"That's all for today," Coach Wilson said. "Gather up the balls and cones. I'll see you tomorrow."

Gabriella started toward the goal to pick up the extra balls, but Coach Wilson stopped her.

"Can I have a word?" Coach Wilson asked.

Gabriella nodded.

Coach waited for the other girls to move away. "Is everything okay?" she asked. "You seem a little off today."

Gabriella sighed. "Something bad happened," she said. "Not end-of-the-world bad but still pretty bad."

"Is there something I can do to help?" Coach Wilson asked.

Gabriella thought about that for a moment. She didn't know if Coach Wilson could help but figured it couldn't hurt to tell her. So she told her coach the whole story.

Coach Wilson listened carefully while Gabriella told her about the backpack, Shaune, and the missing medal. When Gabriella finished, Coach Wilson thought for a moment.

"What are you going to do?" she asked Gabriella.

The question caught Gabriella off guard.

"I, uh, don't really know," she answered. "I was sort of hoping you might have some suggestions."

"Well," Coach Wilson said, "there's not a lot I can do, but I can suggest something you should do."

"Great," Gabriella said. "What's that?"

"You're going to need to tell Shaune what happened," Coach Wilson said. "As for finding the medal, I can't exactly search every student in school. But if you have any ideas about who might have taken the medal, I can have a talk with them."

"That might really help," Gabriella said. "Thanks."

"Don't mention it."

Gabriella jogged across the field to gather up her gear. She wasn't sure how to find the thief. But as she gathered up the balls, she started putting together a plan.

CHAPTER 4

SUSPECTS

Gabriella got up early the next morning and rode her bike to school. Not many students were on campus yet, but she hoped Serena would be there. She found Serena alone in the robotics lab. She stood over a small robot in the middle of the workshop floor.

"This is Pelican 7," Serena said. "It's the team's newest robot and probably the best one we have ever made."

"It looks cool," Gabriella said.

"It *is* cool," Serena replied. "It has proximity detectors, two built-in cameras, and quad core processors that will allow it to perform multiple calculations at the same time. I think we'll win a lot of competitions with this little guy."

"What's your position on the team?" Gabriella asked.

"We don't really have positions," Serena said. "We have roles. I'm the media manager. I'm responsible for documenting the process we go through to create and program the robot. Then I create posters to display at the competitions."

"That sounds really cool," Gabriella said.

Serena snapped a few more pictures of the robot.

"My parents made me join the team," Serena said. "I didn't think I'd like it, but it's actually pretty fun."

Serena moved to the other side of the robot and snapped a picture.

"I'm guessing you didn't come here to talk about robots," she said.

"Not really," Gabriella admitted. "I was wondering if you thought any more about who might have taken the medal."

"I did," Serena said. "Let me download these pictures while we talk."

She crossed the room and sat at a computer terminal. She plugged the camera into a small cable attached to the computer.

"Like I told you yesterday," Serena said. "I got here first and started setting up. But I didn't find out it was your backpack until later. There were other people here by then."

"Do you remember who?" Gabriella asked.

Serena nodded.

"I think so," she said. "Mia got here not long after I did. Then Kyle Robinson showed up. He said he wanted to get ideas for a story for the school paper. After Kyle, Mrs. Warren showed up. She's the faculty sponsor for the team. And Raquel Glass came in with her."

"Raquel, the student council president?" Gabriella asked.

"Yeah, she's the one who got us our new uniforms," Serena said. "She comes by to see how the team is doing. She's quite the politician."

"Okay," Gabriella said. "Mia, Kyle, Mrs. Warren, and Raquel. Anybody else?"

Serena thought for a moment and then shook her head.

"I'm pretty sure that's all," she said. "I don't remember anybody else. Everyone else came after."

"That gives us four suspects," Gabriella said. "Even though I can't imagine Mrs. Warren took the medal."

"I doubt it." Serena agreed. "Plus, she came in and sat at her desk. I don't think she ever got up."

"Then three suspects," Gabriella said. "I'll talk to all three, then see if I can figure out who the thief is."

"I can help," Serena offered. "I feel really bad about this."

"Thanks," Gabriella said. "I could use the help. Who should we start with?"

"Let's start with Kyle," Serena suggested.

"Okay," Gabriella said. "Why Kyle?"

Serena laughed. "You've never seen his website, have you?"

Gabriella *had* seen his website. It was called Robinson's Reckoning, and he used it to publish stories the school paper refused to print. He had published stories about everything from what was in the cafeteria's tuna surprise to who pulled what prank on whom.

He was also known to cause problems at the school so he could then write about them. Gabriella knew that Kyle had ended up in the principal's office more than once because of his website.

"You think he would really put this on his website?" Gabriella asked.

"Well," Serena said, "there's only one way to find out."

CHAPTER 5

LIBRARY

Gabriella met Serena outside the school library at lunchtime. They knew Kyle usually spent lunch using the library computers to work on his website. They hoped they'd find him there.

The library was nearly deserted. Gabriella and Serena walked through the shelves of books to the back of the library. Along the wall, the school had placed a row of tables with several computers. Kyle sat at the computer on the end, typing on the keyboard and eating a sandwich.

"I don't think you're supposed to be eating in here," Serena said.

Kyle smiled and took a large bite of his sandwich.

"There's no one here to stop me," he said. He looked at Gabriella. "Hey, superstar, how about an interview for the school paper?"

"I didn't realize the school paper published your stuff," Gabriella said with a smile.

"That hurts," Kyle said with a fake hurt look. "Besides, if they don't publish it, I can always put it on Robinson's Reckonings."

"I'll pass," Gabriella said. "I actually need to ask you some questions."

"That's interesting," Kyle said. "You want me to answer your questions but don't want to answer mine. I'm not sure how I feel about that."

"Look, Kyle," Serena said. "This is really important. You can answer Gabriella's questions here or in the principal's office. Your choice."

Kyle held his hands up in surrender.

"Okay, okay," he said. "I was just messing around. What do you need to know?"

"You were in the robotics lab yesterday after school, right?" Gabriella asked.

Kyle nodded. "Yes," he said. "I wanted to see if I could get some story ideas for the paper."

"What did you come up with?" Serena asked.

"Nothing really," Kyle replied. "To be honest, I wasn't really sure what was going on."

"When did you get there?" Gabriella asked.

"I don't really know," Kyle said. "Right after school, I guess. There weren't many people there yet."

"Do you remember who was there?" Gabriella asked.

Kyle thought about the question and then pointed at Serena.

"Just her," he said. "And Mia. Everyone else came after that."

"Did you see the medal Serena had in the backpack?" Gabriella asked.

"Not up close," Kyle said. "I heard her say something about grabbing the wrong backpack again, and then she held up a little blue bag and took the medal out."

Kyle's eyes widened.

"What a minute!" he said. "Is that what this is about? Did something happen to the medal?"

"Someone stole it," Serena said.

"You think I stole it?" Kyle asked.

"If you did," Gabriella said, "I won't tell anybody. I just need to get it back."

Kyle shook his head.

"No way!" he said. "It wasn't me. I would never do anything shady like that."

"Come on," Serena said. "You've never created an issue just so you could write about it?"

Kyle looked down at the floor and sighed.

"Okay. Sure, I've sometimes created the news so I'd have something to write about," he said. "But I promise I didn't steal your medal."

"If you didn't," Gabriella asked. "Then who did?"

Kyle shrugged. "I don't know," he said. "But have you talked to Raquel?"

"The student council president?" Gabriella asked.

Kyle nodded. "She showed up after I did, but I'm pretty sure she was there when Serena took out the medal."

"Why would you think she took it?" Gabriella asked.

"I don't know if she did," Kyle said. "But she seemed to be acting a little weird, and she left the robotics lab before I did."

"He might be right," Serena told Gabriella. "Raquel said she wanted to talk to Mia after we finished cleaning up, but when we finished, she was gone."

Kyle folded his arms across his chest.

"That sounds pretty suspicious," he said.

"We need to find Raquel," Gabriella said.

"I can probably help with that," Kyle said. "She always spends her lunch hour in the SAC."

"The student activities center?" Serena asked.

"Yep," Kyle said. "She says she likes to mingle with her fellow students."

Gabriella thanked Kyle, and she and Serena walked to the SAC.

"Do you really think Raquel could be the thief?" Serena asked.

"I don't know," Gabriella said. "But if she is, I have no idea how we're going to prove it."

CHAPTER 6

PRESIDENT

Gabriella and Serena found Raquel sitting at a table in the student activities center. The SAC, as the students called it, was a place for clubs to meet before or after school. During school, students could hang out in the SAC to read or study.

Raquel was watching a video on her phone. On the screen, a man in a dark suit stood at a podium, speaking to a room full of people.

"Can we interrupt you?" Gabriella asked.

Raquel looked up at her and removed an earbud from her ear.

"No problem," she said. "What can I do for the two of you?"

"What is that you're watching?" Serena asked.

"C-SPAN," Raquel replied. "The House of Representatives is debating a bill on infrastructure."

"You're watching that for fun?" Serena asked. She shook her head.

"It's actually pretty interesting," Raquel said. "Plus, I plan to go into politics someday, so I need to stay informed on the issues."

"Wow," Serena said. "That's dedication."

"I get it," Gabriella said. "I want to play in the NWSL one day, so I have to prepare now."

"Exactly," Raquel said. "It's never too early to plan for the future."

"We'd like to ask you a few questions," Gabriella said. "About yesterday."

Raquel paused the video and set her phone on the

table. She looked around, then pointed to the chairs across the table.

"Have a seat," she said.

Gabriella sat down at the table. Raquel sat up straight in her chair and folded her hands on the table in front of her.

"Now," Raquel said. "What happened yesterday?"

"Serena and I accidentally switched backpacks yesterday," Gabriella explained. "While my backpack was in the robotics lab, someone stole something out of it. A medal."

Raquel frowned.

"Are you sure it was stolen?" she asked. "Could it have just fallen out and gotten lost?"

Serena shook her head.

"No way," she said. "I left the backpack in the observation area. I checked the backpack before I left, and it was gone. Someone took it."

"I guess that makes sense," Raquel said. "But I don't understand what you need me for."

"You were in the robotics lab yesterday," Gabriella said.

"Lots of people were there," Raquel said. She shifted a little in her chair. "I don't know how I can be much help. I didn't see anybody take your medal."

"Did you see the medal at all?" Serena asked.

Raquel shrugged.

"I think I heard you say something about a medal," Raquel said. "I don't think I actually saw it."

"You don't think you saw it?" Gabriella asked. "What kind of answer is that?"

Raquel stared across the table at Gabriella. Then she blew out a breath and leaned forward.

"Okay," she whispered. "I saw it. It was in a small blue bag. Happy?"

"Not really," Gabriella said. "Did you take it?"

"Of course not!" Raquel said, louder than she needed to. Several students turned to look at her.

"Look," she said. "I didn't steal your medal, but I can't afford to get caught up in a scandal. Being student council president might not seem like much to a soccer star like you, but it means the world to me."

"I get it," Gabriella said.

"No, you don't," Raquel said. "Kyle Robinson hates me. He'd love to put a story on Robinson's Reckoning calling me a thief. I just hope he doesn't find out you're talking to me."

Gabriella and Serena exchanged a look.

"What?" Raquel asked. "He knows, doesn't he?"

"Yes," Gabriella said. "But I don't think—" She stopped herself. Raquel was probably right.

"I know he was there yesterday," Raquel said.

"We talked to him before coming to find you," Serena said.

"What did he say?" Raquel asked.

"He swears he didn't take the medal," Gabriella said.

"He also says that you were acting strange and left before he did," Serena said.

"See, this is what I'm talking about," Raquel said.

"I was probably acting strange, as he says, because he makes me uncomfortable. Plus, he left before I did."

Gabriella and Serena looked at each other. Gabriella shook her head. Either Kyle or Raquel was lying. But which one? Gabriella had no idea.

The bell rang. Raquel gathered up her things and stood up.

"I have to get to class," she said. "I'm sorry I couldn't be more help."

Raquel walked away before the girls could say anything else.

Serena and Gabriella walked out of the SAC. Serena sighed.

"What now?" she asked.

"I think we need to talk to Mia," Gabriella said. "I can meet you at the robotics lab after practice."

"Okay," Serena said. "Don't worry. We'll find that medal."

Gabriella forced a smile.

"I hope so," she said. *But how?*

CHAPTER 7

PRACTICE

When Gabriella pulled on her cleats for practice that afternoon, she was still preoccupied with thoughts of the medal. Her conversations with Kyle and Raquel hadn't helped much. In fact, they raised more questions than they answered. Still, Gabriella was determined to focus on soccer.

She sprinted the final lap of her warm-up jog, then raced to the goal to run through drills with Neveah.

"Are you okay?" Neveah asked her. "You seemed a little off yesterday."

"I'm better, I think," Gabriella said. "Let's start with turnarounds."

"Okay," Neveah said. "You first."

Gabriella walked to the goal line and stood facing the goal.

"Ready?" Neveah asked.

"Ready."

"Go!" Neveah called.

Gabriella spun around to face Neveah. As she did, Neveah tossed a ball toward the goal. Gabriella lunged for the ball, caught it, and tossed it back. Then she turned around and faced the goal again.

They repeated the drill and, each time, Neveah tossed the ball faster.

"Did you find the medal?" Neveah asked. "Go!"

Gabriella whirled around and caught the ball.

"Not yet," she said. She tossed the ball back to Neveah and turned around again.

46

"What happens if you don't?" Neveah asked. "Go!"

Gabriella hadn't considered that. What would happen if she couldn't find the medal? Shaune would probably be really upset. Gabriella would be embarrassed. Would the media get involved? The police?

"Look out!" Neveah yelled.

Gabriella spun around to catch the ball, but she was too late. The ball was already too close. She tried to raise her hands to block the ball, but she was too slow. The ball hit her right in the face. She fell backward and landed with a thud.

"Owwww," she moaned. She started to sit up.

"Stay down!" Neveah said. "You're bleeding."

Gabriella's lip stung. She touched it with her hand and her hand came away red and wet. Coach Wilson noticed the commotion and ran over.

"What happened?" she asked.

"I was too slow," Gabriella said.

"The ball hit her right in the face," Neveah explained. "Gabriella, I am so sorry."

"It's not your fault," Gabriella said. "I got distracted. I'll be fine."

Coach Wilson helped Gabriella get to her feet.

"It looks like you cut your lip," Coach said. "Come with me. Let's get some ice on it."

Gabriella followed Coach Wilson to the bench and sat down. She could feel her lip starting to swell. Coach Wilson grabbed an ice pack out of a cooler next to the bench and handed it to Gabriella. Gabriella pressed the ice to her lip and winced.

"You're still distracted by the missing medal?" Coach Wilson asked.

Gabriella nodded.

"Do you want to talk about it?"

"I don't want to get anybody in trouble," Gabriella said. "I still don't really know what happened."

Coach sat on the bench next to her.

"Well," she said. "Leave out the names."

"Okay," Gabriella agreed. "There are three suspects. One of them says they saw one of the other suspects acting weird and that that suspect left before everyone else. The second suspect says the first suspect is lying."

"What does the third suspect say?" Coach Wilson asked.

"Nothing," Gabriella said. "We haven't talked to her yet."

"I see," Coach Wilson said. "Well, keep this in mind: Sometimes people aren't lying, they're just mistaken."

"You mean they're both telling the truth?" Gabriella asked.

"I mean they both *think* they're telling the truth," Coach said. "The key is to figure out why each person thinks their version of events is the correct one."

Coach Wilson stood up.

"Keep that ice on your lip," she said. "Once you feel up to it, you can finish your drills with Neveah."

Gabriella nodded. She was already feeling better but wanted a few minutes alone to think.

Why would Kyle think Raquel left first if he was actually the first to leave? Does it even matter?

Gabriella looked toward the goal. Neveah was practicing clearance throws. Without a partner, she had to throw the balls into the goal. Gabriella watched as Neveah scooped up one ball after another and threw each ball into the net.

I'd better get back out there, she thought.

Gabriella jogged back to the goal.

"I'm ready," she told Neveah.

"Okay," Neveah said. "Want to practice goal kicks?"

"Sounds great," Gabriella said. She loved goal kicks. "I'll go first."

"Wait a sec," Neveah said. "I was thinking about something. How well do you know Serena?"

"Not that well," Gabriella said. "We really only talk because we keep switching backpacks. Why?"

"It's probably nothing," Neveah said. "But the captain of the robotics team is my best friend."

"Mia?"

"Right," Neveah said. "We've been friends for years. We used to play soccer together all the time."

"I had no idea," Gabriella said.

"Anyway," Neveah said, "Mia told me that things have been disappearing from the robotics lab lately."

"Disappearing?" Gabriella said. "You mean stolen?"

Neveah nodded.

"It's been going on awhile," she said. "Mia thinks that Serena might be the thief."

CHAPTER 8

TROUBLE

After practice, Gabriella walked to the robotics lab. She wasn't sure what to think. Had Serena really been stealing from the robotics team? Had she also stolen the medal?

Gabriella knew there was only one way to find out. She'd have to confront Serena. She planned to do that as soon as she got to the robotics lab, but when she got there, Gabriella found Mia and Serena waiting for her.

"Serena says you want to talk to me," Mia said.

Gabriella looked at Serena.

"She was getting ready to leave," Serena explained. "I asked her to stay because you needed her help."

"What's this about?" Mia asked. "I don't have much time."

"Someone stole a medal from my backpack yesterday," Gabriella said.

"I know," Mia said. "Serena told me. Switched backpacks. Stolen medal. Three suspects. The whole thing. What do you want from me?"

Gabriella stared at Serena. How much had she told her? And why?

"I think," Serena said. "Since you were here yesterday when the medal disappeared, Gabriella wants to know if you saw anything that might help her figure out what happened."

Mia grunted.

"I was pretty busy," she said. She waved her arms around the room. "The team had my full attention.

I didn't notice anything that would help. I did hear Serena mention the medal. At that point, there was hardly anybody here."

"We talked to Kyle and Raquel already," Gabriella said. "Was anyone else here that you can think of?"

Mia gave the question some thought and shook her head.

"That's it," she said. "Unless you count Mrs. Warren."

"I think we can cross Mrs. Warren off the list," Gabriella said.

"Good call," Mia said. "That just leaves me, Kyle, and Raquel. Oh, and Serena, of course."

Serena flinched, and Gabriella thought about what Neveah had said. *Was Serena really a thief?*

"I have to go," Mia said. "Is there anything else?"

Gabriella couldn't think of anything else to ask.

"I don't think so," she said.

"Well, I'll be here tomorrow if you think of anything," Mia said. She started to leave.

"Wait," Gabriella said. "There is something else. Raquel and Kyle were both here."

"Right," Mia said.

"Do you remember which one of them left first?" Gabriella asked.

Mia frowned. "That's funny," she said. "I could have sworn I saw Kyle leave first but, later on, I noticed Raquel was gone and Kyle was still here. So, I guess Raquel left first."

Mia left, and Serena turned to Gabriella.

"Raquel lied," Serena said. "She's got to be the thief."

Gabriella thought about what Coach Wilson had said.

"I'm not so sure she lied," Gabriella said. "What if she thinks she told us the truth?"

"That's impossible," Serena said. "They can't both be right."

"I'm not saying they're both right," Gabriella said. "But maybe they both think they're right."

"How is that even possible?" Serena asked.

Gabriella thought for a moment and the solution came to her.

"What if Kyle left and came right back?" Gabriella said. "But while he was gone, Raquel left. Raquel would have seen Kyle leaving and thought he left first. Kyle would have come back and seen that Raquel was gone and thought that she left first."

"That would explain what Mia thought she saw," Serena agreed. "But where does that leave us?"

Gabriella wasn't sure. They had gathered a lot of information, but none of it seemed to get her closer to a solution. Plus, there was one more thing weighing on her mind.

"I have a question for you," Gabriella said.

"For me?" Serena asked.

Gabriella nodded.

"Have you been stealing supplies from the robotics team?" she asked.

Serena laughed.

"What?" she said, shaking her head. "That's crazy. Why would I steal anything from here? We're allowed to use it all anyway. Besides, I'm not a thief."

"Did you know things have been disappearing from the lab?" Gabriella asked.

Serena shrugged.

"I've heard Mia complaining about stuff missing, but I didn't pay much attention, to be honest," she said. "How did you hear about it?"

"Well . . ."

"It was Neveah, wasn't it?" Serena said. "She's Mia's best friend. Mia thinks I've been stealing from the team, right?"

Gabriella nodded. "I'm sorry," she said. "I had to ask."

"Why do you care who steals a few random gadgets from the robotics team—" Serena's eyes widened, and she scowled at Gabriella.

"You think I stole your medal," she said. "I've been trying to help you find it!"

"Serena, I'm sorry," Gabriella said. "Neveah told me that, and I didn't know what to think."

"You should have thought that I'm not a thief," Serena spat back. "Good luck finding your medal."

She stomped out of the room and slammed the door behind her.

CHAPTER 9

QUESTIONS

Gabriella rode her bike home and went straight to her room. She lay on her bed and stared up at the ceiling and tried to forget her fight with Serena.

Serena is right. She only tried to help me. I should never have accused her.

Gabriella knew she needed to make things right with Serena. She didn't have her phone number, but she could use the school email system to send her a message.

She sat at her desk and turned on her computer. She logged into her school account and opened her email. She saw that she had a new message. It was from Shaune Covington.

Hi, Gabriella!

I hope you're having a fun time with the U.S. Cup medal. I'm glad I was able to share it with you. Remember to take lots of pictures!

I have some great news. Our publicity manager has arranged for a reporter from ESPN to come with me on Friday when I go to your game. You'll get to be on national TV! How cool is that?

Can't wait to see you play on Friday.

All the best,

Shaune

"This is a disaster," Gabriella said. "I'll have to admit on national TV that I lost Shaune Covington's U.S. Cup medal."

The next morning, Gabriella left early for school, hoping to find Kyle so she could ask him a few more questions. When she rode up to the school, she found Serena waiting for her on the front steps.

"Can we talk?" Serena asked.

Gabriella sat on the steps next to her.

"I want to apologize," Gabriella said. "I never should have accused you of stealing."

"Forget it," Serena said. "You're just trying to do everything you can to find the medal. I shouldn't have gotten so upset. I just . . ." She looked away.

"Just what?" Gabriella asked.

"I don't have many friends," Serena said. "That's part of the reason my parents made me join the robotics team. I was starting to think you and I were becoming friends."

Gabriella nodded. "I'm sorry," she said. "I don't think you're a thief. And you and I are becoming friends."

Serena smiled. "I'd still like to help," she said. "If you need it."

"I need all the help I can get. I want to go see Kyle

again," Gabriella said. "I think there's something he's not telling us."

They found Kyle in his usual spot in front of a computer in the library. He switched off the monitor when he saw them approaching.

"What are you doing?" Serena asked.

"I'm working," Kyle said. "I'm in a hurry, so I don't have time to talk."

"We just have a quick question," Gabriella said.

Kyle groaned.

"Fine," he said. "One question."

"Why didn't you tell us that you left the robotics lab the other day and then came back later?" Gabriella asked. She hoped her hunch would pay off.

Kyle looked from Gabriella to Serena and shook his head.

"How'd you find out?" he asked.

Gabriella smiled. She had been right. If she was right about that, maybe her second hunch was right too.

"How long have you been stealing from the robotics team?" she asked.

Kyle started to protest but thought better of it.

"That's why you left and came back, right?" Gabriella said. "You took something and wanted to get away before anyone noticed."

Kyle glared at Gabriella for a few seconds. Then he laughed.

"Okay," he said. "You caught me."

"What did you take?" Serena asked.

"I guess I might as well show you," Kyle said. He turned back to the computer and hit a button. The monitor blinked to life. The screen displayed an image of a room filled with couches and comfortable chairs. Along the wall was a refrigerator and a small sink. Gabriella leaned in to get a closer look.

"Is that the teacher's lounge?" she asked.

Kyle nodded.

"I borrowed one of the old robotics cameras and set it up in the lounge," he explained.

"You mean you stole it," Serena said.

Kyle shrugged.

"I planned to return it," he said.

"Why are you doing this?" Gabriella asked. "If the teachers find out, you're going to be in a ton of trouble."

"Not this time," Kyle said. "I heard a rumor that some sixth graders were going to set up a prank in the teachers' lounge."

"What kind of prank?" Gabriella asked.

"No idea," Kyle said. "But with this camera, I'll be able to catch them in the act."

"Great," Serena scoffed. "You're a real hero."

"Look, maybe I shouldn't have taken the camera without asking," Kyle said. "But it's for a good cause."

"What else have you taken without asking?" Gabriella asked.

Kyle's face reddened.

"Just small stuff," he said. "Stuff I figured no one would miss. You're not going to report me, are you?"

Serena and Gabriella looked at one another. Serena shrugged.

"You have to return everything you took," she said.

"No problem," Kyle said.

"Including the camera," Serena said.

"Of course," Kyle said.

"And the medal," Gabriella said.

Kyle grimaced. "I can't do that," he said. "I don't have it."

"What did you do with it?" Gabriella asked.

"Nothing," Kyle said. "I never had it. Like I said, I only borrowed things I needed. Stuff that I thought no one would miss. I would never take something like that."

CHAPTER 10

FOCUS

Kyle agreed to meet up with Serena after school to return the things he'd taken from the robotics lab. Gabriella went to soccer practice determined to stay focused and prepare for her big game.

"Are you okay?" Michiko, one of the Pelicans' defenders, asked her as they ran their warm-up laps.

"Of course," Gabriella said. "Why?"

"I usually have to sprint to keep up with you on the last lap," Michiko said. "You're kind of slow today."

Gabriella laughed. "I'm just thinking," she said. "Don't worry, I'm fine."

After running laps, Gabriella and Neveah broke off from the team to complete their drills.

After doing their diving and sliding drills, they did two rounds of turnarounds. After that, they jogged another lap around the field.

"You seem to be feeling better," Neveah said. "Does this mean you found the medal?"

"Not yet," Gabriella said. "But I can't let that get me off my game."

Coach Wilson blew her whistle. "Bring it in, girls!" she shouted.

Gabriella and her teammates gathered around.

"Since we have a game tomorrow," Coach Wilson said, "we're not going to scrimmage today. Instead, we're going to practice defending corner kicks. I'll make the kicks. I want everyone defending. Gabriella, you're in goal first."

The girls jogged to the goal and got in position.

Coach Wilson dropped the ball thirty yards from the goal. Gabriella shouted instructions to get her teammates lined up where she wanted them. She had her teammates form a wall blocking the right side of the goal, so she knew she had to make sure nothing got past her on the left.

Coach Wilson raised her arm and blew her whistle. Then she booted the ball toward the goal.

As Gabriella expected, Coach aimed the ball around the wall. Her shot sailed toward the upper left corner of the goal. Gabriella had positioned herself well to make the save. She timed her jump perfectly and bumped the ball up and over the crossbar. Her teammates cheered.

"Nice save," Coach Wilson called. "Let's line up and do it again."

Coach Wilson tried several more free kicks from various parts of the field. Gabriella stopped every shot.

"Well done, Gabriella," Coach Wilson said. "Neveah, you're up."

After practice, Gabriella gathered up the balls and cones from near the goal and carried them to the bench.

"Nice job today," Coach Wilson told her. "I'm glad to see you've got your focus back."

"It just took some time," Gabriella said.

"Well, I knew you could do it," Coach Wilson said. "You haven't exactly had an easy year. I know your teammates weren't happy when you got the starting spot. But after you went out and played that game in your tennis shoes when your cleats went missing, I knew you could handle anything. Not to mention the saves you made that day you found your jersey covered in paint."

A thought started to form in Gabriella's mind.

"I'm sure they were just silly pranks," Coach Wilson said. "The missing medal probably is too."

"Pranks!" Gabriella said.

"Don't worry," Coach Wilson said. "I'm sure you'll figure out where it went."

"Oh my gosh," Gabriella said. "I do know where it went!"

"You do?"

"Not where it went, exactly," Gabriella said. "But I'm pretty sure I know who took it."

Gabriella raced home and went straight to her room. She paced back and forth and thought everything through. She was sure she was right.

She sat down at her computer, opened her school email account, and sent out five emails. After sending out the last email, she breathed a sigh of relief. Tomorrow, she would have the medal back. She was sure of it.

CHAPTER 11

CONFRONTATION

The next morning, Gabriella parked her bike in front of the school and found Serena waiting for her.

"Are you sure about this?" Serena asked as they entered the school.

Gabriella nodded.

"I'm positive," she said. "I can't believe I didn't figure it out sooner."

They walked together to the robotics lab. Kyle, Raquel, and Mia were there waiting for them.

"What's this about?" Raquel asked. "I told you, I don't want to get involved in any scandals."

"Yeah," Kyle said. "I have a lot of writing to do. Plus, I'm not exactly welcome here."

He looked at Mia, who glared back at him.

"Well," Mia said, "if I didn't have to worry about you stealing everything, then you would be more than welcome. But I can't, so you aren't."

Gabriella held up a hand. "Please," she said. "This won't take long. We're just waiting for one more person."

"Who?" Raquel asked.

"Me?" Neveah said.

They all turned to see Neveah standing in the doorway.

"Am I late?" she asked.

Gabriella shook her head. "No," she said. "Thanks for coming."

"Why is Neveah here?" Mia asked. "She was nowhere near the robotics lab the other day."

"I'll explain," Gabriella said. "First, let's all sit down."

They all pulled chairs into the center of the room and sat.

"There's a lot to cover," Gabriella said. "So, I'll start at the beginning. Serena and I have matching backpacks. We've been getting them mixed up all year."

"I think we all know this already," Kyle said.

"Right," Gabriella said. "What you might not know is that someone has been playing pranks on me. It's been silly stuff mostly. Hiding my cleats, stuff like that. Recently, someone even splashed paint all over my jersey."

"Do you know who did it?" Raquel asked.

"I didn't," Gabriella said. "But I think I do now."

"Can we hurry this up?" Mia asked. "Some of us have stuff to do."

"This week, as you all know, I brought Shaune Covington's U.S. Cup medal to school," Gabriella continued. "It was in my backpack. Serena and I switched backpacks after the assembly, so my backpack came here to the robotics lab."

"I found the medal in the backpack," Serena said. "Then it disappeared before I could return Gabriella's backpack to her. You all are the only people who knew it was here."

"Except me," Neveah said.

"Right," Gabriella said. "And I was so worried about the medal that I didn't ever think it might be connected to the other pranks. Now, I see that it was."

"Whoever has been pranking you also stole the medal?" Neveah asked.

"Right," Gabriella said. "It wasn't hard to figure out who was playing pranks once I stopped and thought about it. The pranks started after Coach Wilson made me the starting goalie. That made a lot of people unhappy."

"Oh wow," Kyle said. He turned to Neveah. "I just remembered, you were the starting goalie last year."

"I was, but—" Neveah started to speak but Kyle cut her off.

"You're an eighth grader. It must have really bugged you to get beaten out by a seventh grader. Did you steal the medal?" he asked.

Neveah sighed. "No, I didn't steal the medal," she said. "Or play any of those other pranks. I didn't care that Coach Wilson made Gabriella the starter. She earned it. Plus, it was a relief."

"A relief?" Serena asked.

Neveah looked around the room.

"I just don't enjoy soccer as much as I used to," she said. "I almost didn't even try out for the team this year, and I'm definitely not bothered that I'm not starting."

"That's easy for you to say now," Raquel said. "Why should we believe you?"

Neveah turned to Gabriella. "You have to believe me," she said. "I didn't steal the medal."

"I know you didn't," Gabriella said. "Mia did."

They all turned to look at Mia, who stared back at them but said nothing.

"Neveah never told you how she felt about soccer," Gabriella said. "So, when I got the starting position, you were upset. You wanted to defend her. You stole my cleats, and you used the paint from the cabinet here to mess up my jersey. When you saw the medal, you knew you had to take it."

Mia balled her hands up into fists.

"It wasn't fair," she said. "Neveah deserved to start. She's always started. She loved the game."

Neveah put her arm around Mia. "I loved the game when I was playing with my best friend," Neveah said. "When you quit playing, it just didn't matter as much to me anymore."

"Mia," Gabriella said, "I get why you did what you did. You were just trying to support your friend. But, please, can I have the medal back?"

Mia stared at Gabriella for a long time. Finally, she walked into the workshop and opened a cabinet.

Silently, she pulled out a small box and brought it to Gabriella.

Gabriella opened the box and pulled out the blue velvet bag. Inside the bag, she found Shaune Covington's medal.

Mia blinked back tears. "I'm sorry," she said. "I really am."

CHAPTER 12

CHAMPIONS

Gabriella wore the medal around her neck for the whole day. After school, she and Serena took a special picture to remember the moment.

Gabriella was still wearing the medal when she got to the soccer field that afternoon. She saw a television truck with a huge antenna parked next to the field. Next to the truck, she saw Shaune Covington chatting with a reporter. Shaune saw Gabriella and waved her over.

"This is Gabriella Carter," Shaune told the reporter. "She's been taking care of my U.S. Cup medal this week. She's also the Pelicans' starting goalie."

Gabriella shook hands with the reporter and hugged Shaune. She took off the medal and handed it to Shaune.

"I see you took good care of it," Shaune said. "I can't wait to see your pictures."

Gabriella grinned.

"Well, I have a lot to tell you about my week," she said.

"Tell me later," Shaune said. "You've got a game to get ready for."

Gabriella trotted onto the field and started warming up with her teammates.

"Did you see who's here?" Layla asked Gabriella. "Shaune Covington. I'm so nervous."

"Don't worry," Gabriella said. "We just have to focus."

Coach Wilson called the girls together.

"Okay, Pelicans," she said. "This is it. Win today, and you're champions."

The girls nodded their heads.

"Also, I know you all saw Shaune Covington is here to watch the game and cheer you on. Make her proud!"

The girls cheered and ran out to line up for the opening kickoff.

Gabriella fist-bumped Neveah and ran to her goal. She touched both posts, then jumped up and tapped the crossbar. She was ready.

"Let's go, Pelicans!" she yelled.

The Pelicans' opponents, the Marauders, were set to kick off. The referee blew her whistle, and the game was on.

The Marauders came forward fast. Their midfielder kicked a long pass down the right side. The Marauders' winger sprinted after it and kicked a crossing pass right in the box where the striker leapt into the air for a header. She headed the ball to the bottom left corner of the goal, but Gabriella was ready. She dove and caught the ball.

"Nice save!" Coach Wilson shouted.

Gabriella jumped up and kicked the ball downfield to start a counter attack. Layla ran under the ball and headed it forward to Kaylee. Kaylee dribbled past a defender and into the box. She passed the ball to Gemma, who kicked it past the diving Marauders' goalie and into the net.

"Gooooaaaaaalllllll!"

The crowd cheered.

"Nice job, Pelicans!" Shaune yelled.

The Marauders kicked off and their midfielder passed the ball all the way back to their goalie. The goalie booted a long pass toward midfield. It soared high in the air. Layla ran under the ball and tried to head it but missed.

The Marauders' striker chased down the ball and raced toward the Pelicans' goal. She was one-on-one with Gabriella. The crowd groaned.

Gabriella raced forward to try to cut off the striker's angle. The striker faked left, then right, but Gabriella stayed focused on the ball. The striker took her shot, and Gabriella dove to block it. She timed it perfectly.

Gabriella punched the ball away from the goal, and it bounced harmlessly out of bounds. The crowd cheered. Layla ran over and gave Gabriella a high five.

"Sorry," Layla said. "I should have had that header."

"Don't worry about it," Gabriella said. "You'll get the next one."

The Pelicans led 1 to 0 until the very end of the game. With time running out, the Marauders stole the ball and sprinted up the field. They passed the ball back and forth until the striker got the ball just outside the penalty box. Michiko attempted a sliding tackle but missed the ball and kicked the striker's shin instead.

The referee's whistle pierced the air. "Free kick!" she shouted.

The crowd groaned. The Marauders would have one last chance to tie the game. Gabriella would need to make the save to secure the Pelicans' win. She shouted directions to her team to get them in position. She built a wall of players between her and the goal. Only the right side of the goal was exposed. She knew she would have to cover that space.

A Marauders midfielder stepped up to take the kick. She raised her arm, and the referee blew her whistle. The midfielder moved forward to kick the ball, and Gabriella leaned toward the exposed area of her goal.

The midfielder kicked the ball, and Gabriella knew right away it wasn't going where she thought. Instead, the ball curled over the wall and toward the goal.

Gabriella changed directions and dove for the ball. She knew she couldn't catch it, but she hoped she could at least slap it away. She stretched both arms out and reached for the ball. The ball hit her fingers, bouncing wide of the goal and out of bounds. The crowd cheered as the referee blew her whistle three times. The game was over!

The Pelicans swarmed around Gabriella to celebrate. She felt a hand on her shoulder and turned around to see Shaune smiling at her. Shaune put her medal around Gabriella's neck.

"I think you've earned the right to wear this a little longer," Shaune said.

"Thanks," Gabriella said. "I'm not sure you'd feel that way if you knew what happened to it this week."

Shaune laughed. "It can't be any worse than the time I lost it for a whole week," she said.

Gabriella grinned. "Maybe I'll tell you about it another time."

Bryan Patrick Avery discovered his love of reading and writing at an early age when he received his first Bobbsey Twins mystery. He writes picture books, chapter books, and graphic novels. His middle-grade story, "The Magic Day Mystery," was published in 2020 in *Super Puzzletastic Mysteries*, an anthology from HarperCollins and the Mystery Writers of America. His debut picture book, *The Freeman Field Photograph*, was published in 2020. Bryan lives in northern California with his family.

GLOSSARY

calculations (kal-kyuh-LAY-shuhns)—use of a mathematical process to determine an outcome

championship (CHAM-pee-uhn-ship)—a series of games or contests to determine a top winner

circuitry (SUR-ki-tree)—the science of creating paths for electrical currents

clean sheet (KLEEN SHEET)—a soccer match in which a team or goalkeeper prevents the other team from scoring

commotion (kuh-MOH-shuhn)–noisy excitement and confusion

infrastructure (IN-fruh-struhk-cher)—the basic equipment and structures needed for a country to function properly

occupy (OK-yuh-pye)—to take or fill up

preoccupied (pree-OK-yuh-pyed)—completely distracted

processor (PROS-es-er)—a part of the computer that handles data

rummage (RUHM-ij)—to dig through and search for something

scandal (SKAN-dl)—something that angers or shocks people because rules or standards are broken

DISCUSSION QUESTIONS

1. After Gabriella and Serena search the robotics lab for the medal and can't find it, Gabriella turns to Coach Wilson for help. Who would you turn to for help if you needed it?

2. At practice, Gabriella is distracted because she hasn't been able to find the medal. Think about a time you've struggled to focus on something you're doing because you were worried about something else. What did you do?

3. Do you think Mia's actions have damaged her relationship with Neveah? What might she do to help repair their friendship?

WRITING PROMPTS

1. If Gabriella had not solved the mystery, she would have needed to confess to Shaune Covington that she had lost the medal. Write a note from Gabriella to Shaune to tell her that the medal is missing. Or write a scene in which Gabriella tells Shaune in person.

2. Imagine you had the opportunity to carry around a special medal or trophy for a week. Write a short article about where you took the medal and whom you shared it with and why.

3. Write a letter of apology from Mia to Gabriella for all the trouble she caused. How would Mia explain her behavior?

FACTS ABOUT SOCCER AND KEEPING GOAL

A soccer field is typically called a "pitch." This is because in England, where the first official leagues were formed, a playing field is known as a pitch.

There is no standard size for a soccer pitch. According to FIFA (Fédération Internationale de Football Association), the pitch must be 110–120 yards long by 70–80 yards wide.

While the size of the pitch may vary, the size of the goal cannot. Every goal must be 8 yards wide and 8 feet tall.

Briana Scurry, former goalkeeper for the U.S. Women's National Team, holds the record for the most clean sheets (a match without giving up a goal) in a World Cup career with ten.

The two posts and the crossbar of each goal must be painted white. No other colors are allowed.

American goalkeeper Tim Howard holds the record for most saves in a World Cup game. He saved sixteen shots against Belgium in the 2014 World Cup in Brazil.

Goalkeepers Nadine Angerer of Germany and Hope Solo of the United States share the record for the most consecutive minutes without conceding a goal. The record is 540 minutes or nine hours!

Nadine Angerer also set the record for fewest goals conceded in a tournament: zero! In Germany's 2007 World Cup championship run, Nadine didn't give up a single goal for the entire tournament.

SOLVE ALL THE SPORTS MYSTERIES!

JAKE MADDOX JV MYSTERIES

CHEER
FEARS

JAKE MADDOX JV MYSTERIES

OFF
BASE

JAKE MADDOX JV MYSTERIES

SOCCER
SUSPICIONS

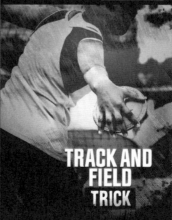

JAKE MADDOX JV MYSTERIES

TRACK AND FIELD
TRICK